AF746340

Captain Thunderbolt's Recital

Jane Jolly &
Liz Duthie

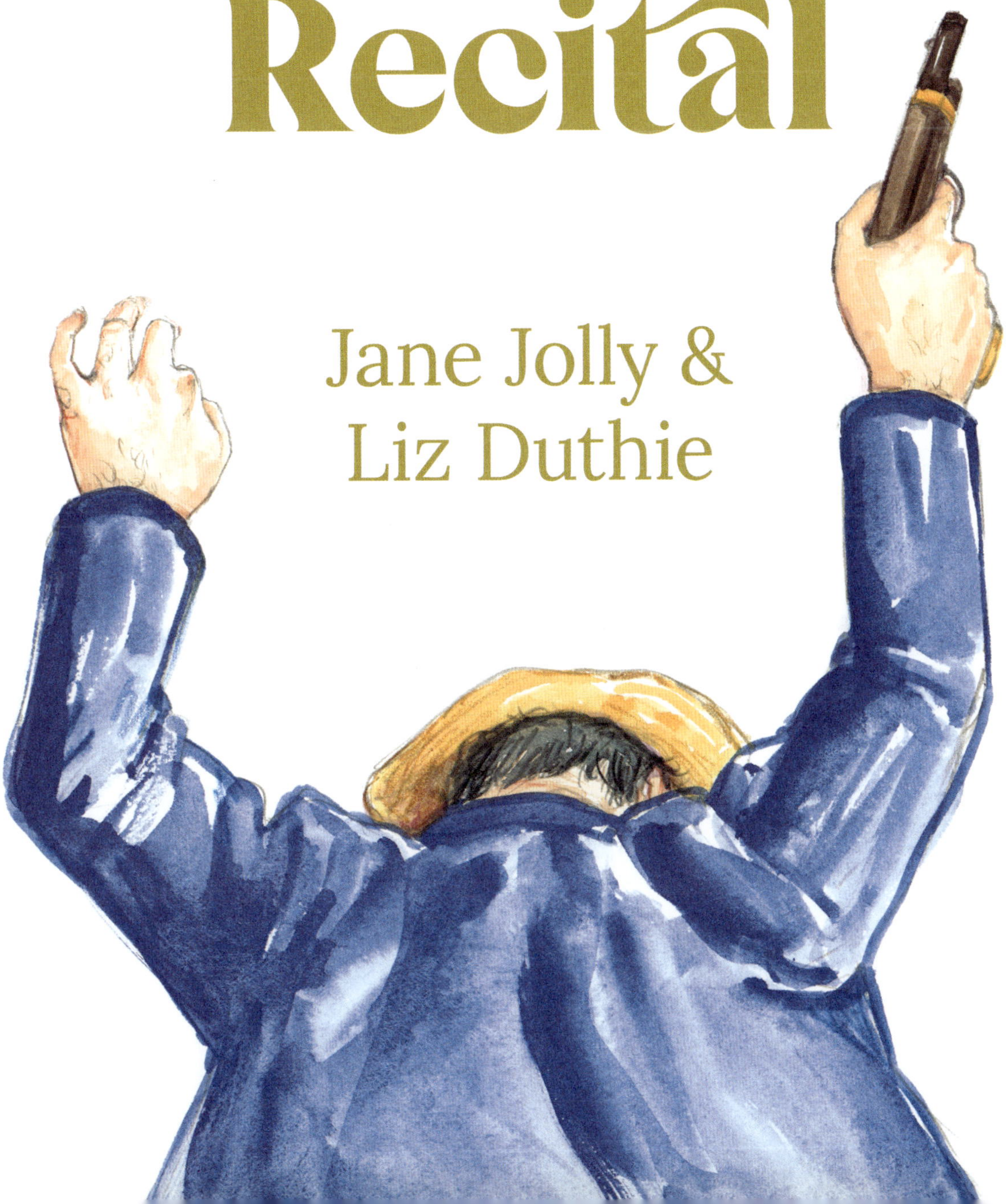

CELEBRATING
NATIONAL LIBRARY OF AUSTRALIA PUBLISHING
50 YEARS

Captain Thunderbolt emerged from his hideout. “What a beautiful day!” he sang. He picked up his tin whistle and played a jig.

“A glorious day for a ride, Spirit my old friend,” said Thunderbolt and he mounted his faithful horse.

He sang loudly as they cantered through the bush. And then a thought occurred to him. He felt his pouch. It was empty. Not even a shilling.

"We need to find us some money, Spirit, so we can celebrate this glorious day and buy me a nice hot meal and you a sweet piece of sugar loaf."

Captain Thunderbolt led Spirit behind a large granite boulder. Before long he spied a creaky wagon making its way along the rough track. The two horses pulling it were slow and skinny. Sitting on top of the wagon were four moustachioed men. One was singing in a strange language.

"Stop there! I am Thunderbolt! The King of the Bush!" cried the bushranger as he rode in front of the cart.

Thunderbolt fired a shot from his revolver. *Whizz!* It flew past their ears.

The men quivered and put up their hands.

"Oh! Ho! What have we here?" said Thunderbolt as he looked into the wagon.

There lay the battered and bruised instruments of a brass band. A drum. A cornet. A trombone. A bassoon. A tuba. And a flugelhorn.

"Well, well, well. It's a band! Play me some music!" he ordered. "But before you begin I want all of your money! You must pay me to listen," he laughed.

The four men climbed slowly down from the wagon. Shaking, they handed over their hard-earned pounds and then passed around their instruments.

Just as he was stuffing
the money into his pouch,
Thunderbolt heard the sound
of horses fast approaching.

"Quick! Hide me under your drum
or things will be worse for you all."

A troop of policemen rode up in a cloud of dust.
"Have you seen the bushranger Thunderbolt?" they called.

“N … no … no-one,” stuttered Ernst.
“We have just stopped for a rest.”

The police raced off and when the sound of the horses had disappeared Thunderbolt's head popped up like a jack-in-the-box.

“Well done lads. You’ll be thankful one day.
I promise. Now off you go then. Play me a tune.
What about you begin with *The Blue Danube Waltz*?”

Ernst fumbled with his bassoon. His fingers shook as he lifted it and began to play.

Brrroo! Brrroo! Brrroo! Brrroo!

Brrroo!

Peter put the trombone to his lips. His moustache quivered as he took a breath.

Woomp! Woomp!
Woomp! Wah!

The trombone slide moved in and out as he played.

Woomp!

Jacob picked up his flugelhorn with trembling hands. His eyebrows went up and down as he concentrated.

Praap! Praap! Praap! Praap!

Praap!

Oom Pah Pah!

Johannes nervously held the tuba to his mouth. The first note came out as a *squark*! He took a slow breath and began again. His eyes popped as he blew hard. The deep notes shuddered.

Oom Pah Pah! Oom Pah Pah!

Thunderbolt conducted the musicians using his revolver as a baton. He began to hum along with the music and then he waltzed around the wagon.

"Once again! But this time more softly. More slowly," said Thunderbolt with dreamy eyes.

The men played on and Thunderbolt applauded.

They played rousing marching music and romantic ballroom music.

After they finished, Johannes begged Captain Thunderbolt:
"Please don't take our money. We are poor men."

"Fear not. I am only borrowing it!" said Thunderbolt.
"Once I get myself a winning racehorse I will pay you all back.
Give me your names and addresses."
The men raised their eyebrows.
They didn't believe him for one minute.

Johannes scribbled down
their details, his eyebrows
still firmly raised.

"One last song before I go,"
said Thunderbolt.
"Make it a jolly old one."

Johannes lifted his tuba,
and tapping his foot,
began a German polka.

Rumpa-tum! Rumpa-tum!
Tum! Tum! Tum!

Thunderbolt roared with laughter
and danced a merry jig.

“Thankyou for the wonderful music. Before I leave, let me play *you* a tune. This is my dear mama’s favourite.” And with that he pulled out his tin whistle and played a cheerful little ditty.

At the end he bowed with a flourish. "Good afternoon and *auf wiedersehen*," he said and jumped onto his horse. "Gee up Spirit!" He rode off into the bush, disappearing as quickly as he had appeared.

The bandsmen breathed a sigh of relief.
With wobbly legs they climbed aboard
their wagon and set off for home.

Sure enough, weeks later, the men were delivered postal orders to the amount of fifty pounds—the exact amount Thunderbolt had taken from them.

Just one week earlier, a horse trainer had been robbed of his winnings … by a rogue called Thunderbolt!

A TRUE STORY

Bushranging began in Australia early after the British arrived in 1788. Most bushrangers were escaped convicts and used to hide out in and 'range' across the Australian bush. It is thought there could have been up to 2,000 bushrangers, including a few women. Many were considered dangerous criminals and there were frequent shoot-outs between bushrangers and the police.

Bushrangers often had strange names. Bluecap got his name because he would wear a blue cloth over his eyes to protect them from the sunlight. Captain Moonlite gave himself that name; he wore a mask and cloak when robbing people. Captain Thunderbolt got his name after bursting through a door, which police said sounded like a thunderbolt.

The Gold Rush was a profitable time to be a bushranger. There were no banks in those days and lone travellers, small groups and mail coaches were easy targets because of the isolated sites of the goldfields and the lack of police. Large amounts of gold were often being transported. It was easy to rob and it was also easy to exchange gold for cash. When new roads and railways were built, transport became faster and much safer and this led to the end of the bushranging era in the 1880s.

Captain Thunderbolt was born in 1835. He was the son of a convict and the youngest of ten children. His real name was Frederick Wordsworth Ward. He worked as a horse breaker and a drover, and was sent to prison twice for stealing a horse.

In 1862, he escaped and became known as the 'gentleman bushranger'. It is said he never shot anyone. Thunderbolt did most of his bushranging in northern New South Wales, where he robbed mailmen, travellers, inns, stores and stations. He also stole more than 40 thoroughbred racehorses.

Thunderbolt sometimes worked together with his partner, Mary Ann Bugg. Mary Ann's father was an ex-convict and her mother was an Aboriginal woman, probably from the Worimi Nation. She was a skilled scout, and it is believed Thunderbolt was able to evade capture for so long because of Mary Ann's knowledge of the land.

Johannes Wirth arrived in Australia from Bavaria in Germany in 1855 and formed Wirth's German Brass Band with his brothers, Jacob and Peter, and another man, Ernst. The band travelled the district around Tamworth in a horse-pulled wagonette, playing at processions, parties and balls. This encounter is based on a true story!

For Kim C. We would have made good bushrangers! JJ
For Lila, Iris, Neve and Simon with love. LD

Published by National Library of Australia Publishing
Canberra ACT 2600

ISBN: 9781922507464

© National Library of Australia 2023
Text © Jane Jolly 2023
Illustrations © Liz Duthie 2023

The National Library of Australia acknowledges Australia's First Nations Peoples—the First Australians—as the Traditional Owners and Custodians of this land and gives respect to the Elders—past and present—and through them to all Australian Aboriginal and Torres Strait Islander people.

This book is copyright in all countries subscribing to the Berne Convention. Apart from any fair dealing for the purpose of research and study, criticism or review, as permitted under the Copyright Act 1968, no part may be reproduced by any process without written permission. Enquiries should be made to the publisher.

Publisher: Lauren Smith
Editor: Amelia Hartney
Designer: Hannah Janzen
Image coordinator: Jemma Posch
Printed in China by C&C Offset Printing Co. Ltd on FSC®-certified paper.

Find out more about NLA Publishing at nla.gov.au/national-library-publishing.
Teachers' notes for this book are available at publishing.nla.gov.au/pages/teachers-notes.do.

NATIONAL LIBRARY OF AUSTRALIA

A catalogue record for this book is available from the National Library of Australia

FSC www.fsc.org MIX Paper | Supporting responsible forestry FSC® C008047